Cover design and hand lettering by Mirelle Ortega
Book design by Amanda Bartlett

9781223186849 English hardcover
9781223186863 English ebook

Published by Paw Prints Publishing
PawPrintsPublishing.com
Printed in China

THE MUSEUM LIVES IN ME

MISS EDMONIA'S CLASS OF WILDFIRES

WRITTEN BY
VICTORIA SCOTT-MILLER

ILLUSTRATED BY
FRANCISCO SANTOYO

PAW PRINTS
PUBLISHING
PAWPRINTSPUBLISHING.COM

Class field trips were always fun,
but Miss Edmonia took trips to the
art museum *very* seriously.

Clap, clap.
"Ahem! Class, what are we?"
"**Wildfires!**" the children shouted.

"And what does that mean?" asked Miss Edmonia.

"We are
Wise,
Intelligent,
Lovable,
Determined,
Fiercely
Innovative,
Respectful,
Exuberant
Scholars."

"Very good, Wildfires!" said Miss Edmonia.

"Now, onward and upward!"

"What a beautiful walk toward the museum," said Miss Edmonia.
"Now, let's turn on our listening ears and open our eyes wide.
I can tell you're excited. So, I won't make you wait.
Here's your paper and pencil. Now, let's take a look at the art;
let's find your traits!"

"Honesty, bravery, strength, or compassion?
As we walk around, what grabs your attention?
Class, open your hearts to the wonders you'll see
as we explore these beautiful galleries.
Are there any questions before we enter?"

"May I sit down?"

"Where's the bathroom?"

"Can we take the art home?"

And like shooting stars blazing across the sky,
Miss Edmonia answered their questions all at once:
"Yes. If you need it, give your legs a rest.
The bathroom is down the hall and to the left.
And no. It's important that art reflects what's
within *and* those around.
If we took it home, it would not be found."

Attilo sat on the leather bench.
Kara-Clementine walked from the corridor
to sit next to him.

"Hey, Attilo?" she asked. "What's the matter?"

"I think museums are boring," Attilo said. "I wish I could play my
video game right now, play soccer. Listen to my music in bed.
Anything but this."

"Trust me, I understand exactly what you mean.
How you feel about the museum
is how I feel about the violin.
But my parents make me play it anyway.
I'd much rather be doing this!"
And she pointed to her hand-painted shoes.

Then, Kara-Clementine hopped off the
bench and rounded the bend, toward a new adventure . . .
Miss Edmonia's voice faded into the distance, leaving only the screech
of sneakers on the wood floor as little feet shuffled from piece to piece.

Soon, Kara-Clementine stopped in her tracks.
Her jaw dropped and her eyes widened as she looked up, mesmerized.
She titled her head side to side.
The lines and shadowing began to stretch beyond the walls of the canvas.
The woman in the painting stared at Kara-Clementine.
Fierce.

Seeing Kara-Clementine's excitement, Attilo got up and, headphones on, joined his class to look at the art before his boredom grew.

He weaved this way and that and paused at a boxing scene. "Well, this isn't boring!" he thought.

He then came to a painting
of a jazz ensemble.
Oranges, teals, and golds.

As he marveled at the image, all that
movement, the music in his ears
grew muffled and was replaced by the
beautiful burst of a brassy trumpet.
As he closed his eyes, this new music
transported him to a dazzling French
Quarter. He stood in place, swaying
from side to side.

Miss Edmonia exclaimed:
"Let's keep up, class! No lagging behind.
Ask if you have questions. I am here to guide!"

Attilo quickly snapped out of his
musical trance and walked over to
his class at the entrance of the new
modern light installation.

"Look at this," cried Kara-Clementine. "It's magical!"

"This is art, too?" thought Attilo. It felt like being in one of his video games.

"It's an infinity of stars!"
Kara-Clementine continued.
Attilo helped fellow Wildfire Tanner
step inside the illuminated
room. "Watch your feet,"
he told him, and took his hand.
Then he
watched
as Tanner skipped down
the dim corridor to the
rest of his classmates, who
were now making funny faces
at one another.

Attilo stood still, reflecting, as his class began
moving toward the next gallery.
Everything began to slow down, and it was
in this stillness that he was reminded of how
easy it was to help his classmates, family, and
even community members.

Realizing he felt most comfortable when
collaborating or helping others, he thought
of a character trait that he could not yet say
aloud. With a deep sigh, he shrugged his
shoulders and moved along.

Kara-Clementine had waited for Attilo.
"Guess what? I found my trait! I'm a leader!"

"Don't you think you're creative, too?" Attilo asked.
"Just look at your shoes. They've got cardboard wings!"

"I can see that! Thanks, Attilo," said Kara-Clementine. "After seeing the
confident woman in that painting, I feel anything is possible for me."

"I can't wait to show my parents how art and music go hand in hand; both
take creativity and leadership! What about you? What's your trait?"

"I don't know yet," Attilo answered
with a slight pause in his voice.

"I'm excited, class, to learn your traits.
Just a few more stops to navigate.
We'll visit ancient Egypt, Greece, Rome,
Italy, and then finish at Rodin.
Did you know his amazing sculptures
were all made by hand?!"

The class began to weave throughout the galleries once more. Some pointed at the bust of the cat goddess Sekhmet, as others giggled at the nose on the portrait of the emperor Marcus Aurelius. They finally arrived at the sculptures of Auguste Rodin.

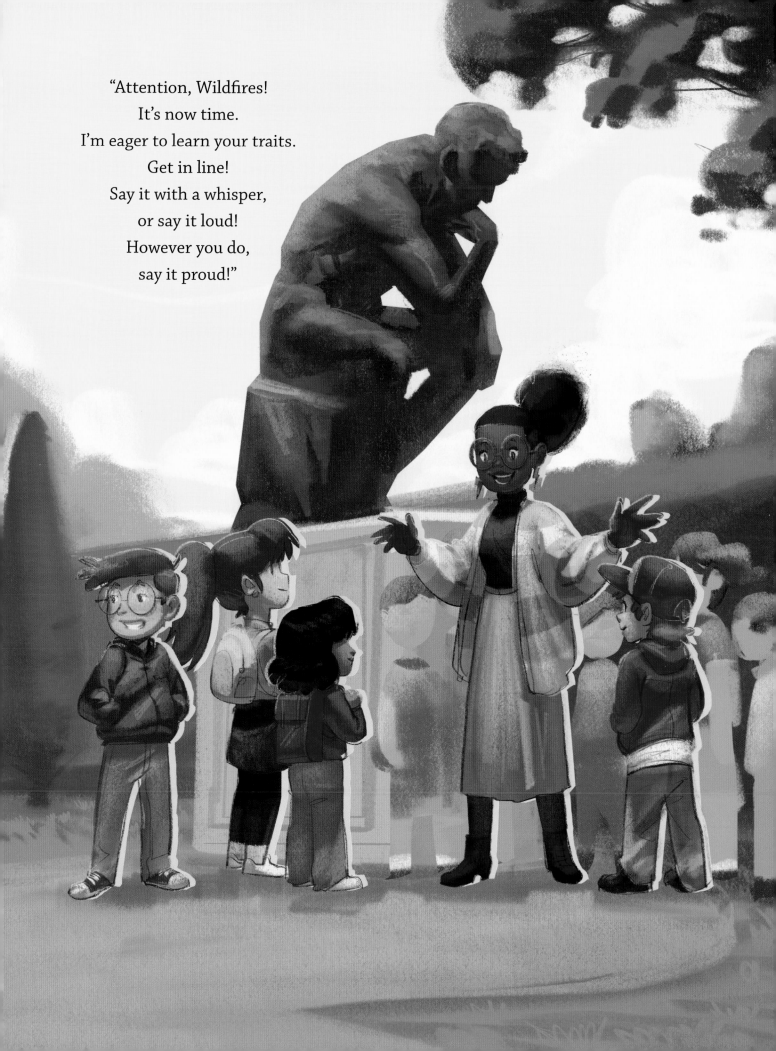

"Attention, Wildfires!
It's now time.
I'm eager to learn your traits.
Get in line!
Say it with a whisper,
or say it loud!
However you do,
say it proud!"

"Edwin, Kara-Clementine, Attilo . . . you go first!
Tell us the discoveries you've unearthed."

Edwin shouted,
"I AM **CURIOUS**!"

"You are a Courageous,

Upbeat,

Radiant,

Innovative,

Optimistic,

Unique

Star!"

"I AM . . . I AM . . . Never mind . . ."
Attilo slumped and walked toward Miss Edmonia.

"Go on, Attilo," Miss Edmonia said encouragingly.

"I . . . AM . . . **KIND** . . . ?!" said Attilo.

"Yes! Yes! You are a Knowledgeable,

Inspiring,

Noble

Dreamer."

One by one, the Wildfires shared their traits that they
uncovered within the museum's collection.
"Thank you all for sharing!" said Miss Edmonia.
"Now, gather around, my Wildfires, and
let's do a Rodin pose. Is everyone ready?"

"Yes!" the class shouted joyously.

"All right. Smile, and on the count of three, say:
'The Museum Lives in Me!'"

"And whether it's bravery, curiosity, compassion, or grit, a museum's collection should reflect all parts of you . . . Your gifts, tenacity, goodness, the creativity in all that you do.

"So always remember that no matter your race, color, gender, or creed, art resides inside of you; you make the gallery."